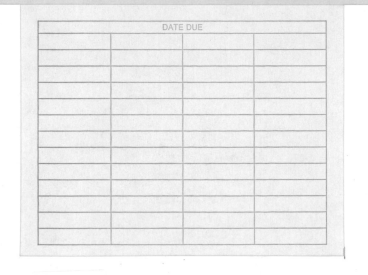

JAMES MARSH

BIZARRE BIRDS & BEASTS

DIAL BOOKS
NEW YORK

DAWN CHORUS

When the sun turns night to day
An orchestra begins to play.
The hummingbird soon draws its bow
To make a tune that's soft and low.
While in the reeds a feathered choir
Sounds like a sax or flute or lyre.
Before the sun has risen high,
Away the music-makers fly.

James Marsh

MONKEY BUSINESS

Monkey in a flying suit
Contemplates his aircraft route.
Goggles for his eyes and nose
Leather trousers to his toes.
Without a doubt, this monkey's smart —
If you can't fly, then dress the part.

CLEVER CATS

Cats are crafty, cats are wise,
Cats can even use disguise —
Though sometimes they may look absurd
Just to fool the smallest bird.

Cats are cunning, cats are sly,
Cats will rarely tell you why,
Skulking all around the house,
They tease and scare each little mouse.

THE PELICAN'S BILL

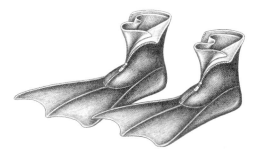

A special bill is the pelican's pride,
It likes to pack its lunch inside.
Scooping fish just like a net,
Why does it let its feet get wet?

Imagine catching all those fish
Without a need for plate or dish.
Or crunching, munching, all day long
Without a moment for a song.

FROG PRINCE

An agile prince of the lily pad
Is likely to get hopping mad
If he isn't left alone
On his gently floating throne.
Since catching gnats in solitude
Better suits his royal mood.

Best not to try and kiss a frog
Just let him reign, for it's his bog.

SPOT THE LION

The king of beasts is noted for
His handsome mane and fearsome roar.
But when he gets a rash or flu,
He shows it just as much as you.

Take care if tracking such a creature,
With crimson spots as his main feature,
Since you might whet his appetite
He'll spot *you* — then take a bite!

SEA TURTLE

The turtle glides with flippers spread
Over the wide ocean bed.
When it nests, it rests on sand
And then its babies hatch on land.
The little turtles soon emerge
And take to sea, at Nature's urge.

TIGER MOTHS

Graceful prowlers of the air —
Tiger moths are truly rare.
Hunting through the forests deep
While the world is fast asleep.
Moths are magical in flight,
Their tawny wings enhance the night.

CHAMELEON CAMOUFLAGE

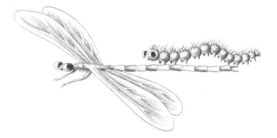

The chameleon seems to match its skin
To whatever place it's in....
Whether blue or yellow or red or green
The tricky lizard can't be seen.
(This proves useful when a fly
Perches on a branch nearby.)

A dragonfly will never see
Its enemy in time to flee
The tongue darts out, and with a snap!
Dinner's caught in a sticky trap.

THE WISE OWL

High up a tree, the owl writes
Through long and chilly winter nights.
Sitting still without a sound,
Watching everything around.
Its tufted head in darkness peers
Taking note of what it hears.
Knowledge isn't hard to earn —
"The more you listen, the more you learn."

BEAR SKIN

Polar bear on an icy floe,
Cozy in the land of snow,
Warm within his coat of fur,
There's little need for him to stir.

If you'd like some wintry wear,
Please think twice before you dare
To choose a fur — remember, too,
It suits him more than it suits you!

JEWELED PARROT

In jungles deep this bird is queen,
Her mantle is of emerald green.
She looks through bright and ruby eyes,
Her kingdom is a paradise.

High in the forest canopy
She wings her way from tree to tree.
Freedom is the parrot's due
So please don't cage her in a zoo.

COW DREAMS

On sunny meadows the cow can graze
And so pass long, hot summer days.
(Sitting under shady boughs
Is the sole relief for cows.)
But what if they should get the notion
To take a break beside the ocean?
Of such vacations cows might dream…
Yet we'd soon miss the milk and cream!

FLYING FISH

When sleepy fishermen close their eyes
Their hopes, like flying fish, can rise.
And soaring upward in the sky
They know just what it is to fly.

FUTURE ARK

Imagine a world where humans would
Do their best for the planet's good:
Water pure and forests fair—
No pollution to kill the air.
Can we change our ways much faster
And avoid complete disaster?

For without space to live in peace
The animals will soon decrease
Then disappear without a trace—
Could robot creatures take their place?
There isn't time to wait and see…
The microchip can't make a tree.

To Mum & Dad, the birds & bees

First published in the United States 1991 by
Dial Books
A Division of Penguin Books USA Inc.
375 Hudson Street
New York, New York 10014

Published in Great Britain 1991 by
Pavilion Books Limited
Copyright © 1991 by James Marsh

Designed and produced by
Russell Ash and Bernard Higton
All rights reserved
Printed and bound in Italy by Arnoldo Mondadori
First Edition
1 3 5 7 9 10 8 6 4 2

Library of Congress Cataloging in Publication Data
Marsh, James, 1946–
Bizarre birds & beasts
written and illustrated by James Marsh.
p.   cm.
Summary: A collection of light verse
about creatures both real and imaginary.
ISBN 0-8037-1046-1
1. Animals—Juvenile poetry.   2. Children's poetry, English.
1. Animals—Poetry. 2. English poetry.   I. Title. II. Title:
Bizarre birds and beasts.
PR6063.A6598B5 1991   821'.914—dc20   91–8236 CIP   AC